Hiding Hetty

'Hiding Hetty'
An original concept by Jenny Moore
© Jenny Moore 2023

Illustrated by Kristen Humphrey

Published by MAVERICK ARTS PUBLISHING LTD
Studio 11, City Business Centre, 6 Brighton Road,
Horsham, West Sussex, RH13 5BB
© Maverick Arts Publishing Limited May 2023
+44 (0)1403 256941

A CIP catalogue record for this book is available at the British Library.

ISBN 978-1-84886-954-7

www.maverickbooks.co.uk

This book is rated as: Green Band (Guided Reading)
It follows the requirements for Phase 5 phonics.
Most words are decodable, and any non-decodable words are familiar,
supported by the context and/or represented in the artwork.

Hiding Hetty

By Jenny Moore

Illustrated by Kristen Humphrey

Hetty and Skip are playing hide-and-seek.

Hetty counts first.

"...Nineteen, twenty... Here I come!"

Hetty peeks round the tree.

She checks under the flowers.

Where is Skip?

He is not at the pond.

He is not in the hedge.

He is not down his rabbit hole.

Hetty frowns. "I give up. Where are you?"

Two long ears pop up from the corn.

"Boo!" shouts Skip. "I win!"

"Now I will count while you hide," Skip tells Hetty.

Hetty trots off, looking for a good place.

But the tree is too thin.

Her bottom sticks out the sides!

The wall is too low.

Her horns stick out the top.

She is too big to hide under the flowers.

She is too big to hide in the hedge.

'I am no good at playing this game,'

Hetty thinks. But then she spots something.

Hetty grins. "Perfect! Skip will never find me in there!"

"...Nineteen, twenty... Here I come!" shouts Skip. 'It will not be hard to find a big cow like Hetty,' he thinks.

He looks in the flowers.

He checks in the hedge.

He peeks behind the tree.

He sneaks under the fence...

Skip stares at the field. "How will I find a big cow like Hetty in here?"

"I give up!" Skip shouts.

"Where are you?"

Two long horns pop up from the crowd of cows.

Hetty smiles. "Moo! I win!"

Skip grins back at her.

"That was a fantastic place to hide! You are so good at this game!"

Quiz

1. Who counts first?
a) Skip
b) A bird
c) Hetty

2. Where does Skip hide?
a) In the corn
b) In the flowers
c) In a bush

3. Why can't Hetty hide behind the wall?
a) Her bottom sticks out the side
b) She is too big
c) Her horns stick out the top

4. Why can't Hetty hide in the rabbit hole?
a) It is too dark
b) She is too big
c) It is full of carrots

5. Where does Hetty hide?
a) In the corn
b) In a crowd of cows
c) Behind a tree

Turn over for answers

Book Bands for Guided Reading

The Institute of Education book banding system is a scale of colours that reflects the various levels of reading difficulty. The bands are assigned by taking into account the content, the language style, the layout and phonics. Word, phrase and sentence level work is also taken into consideration.

Maverick Early Readers are a bright, attractive range of books covering the pink to white bands. All of these books have been book banded for guided reading to the industry standard and edited by a leading educational consultant.

To view the whole Maverick Readers scheme, visit our website at www.maverickearlyreaders.com

Or scan the QR code above to view our scheme instantly!

Quiz Answers: 1c, 2a, 3c, 4b, 5b